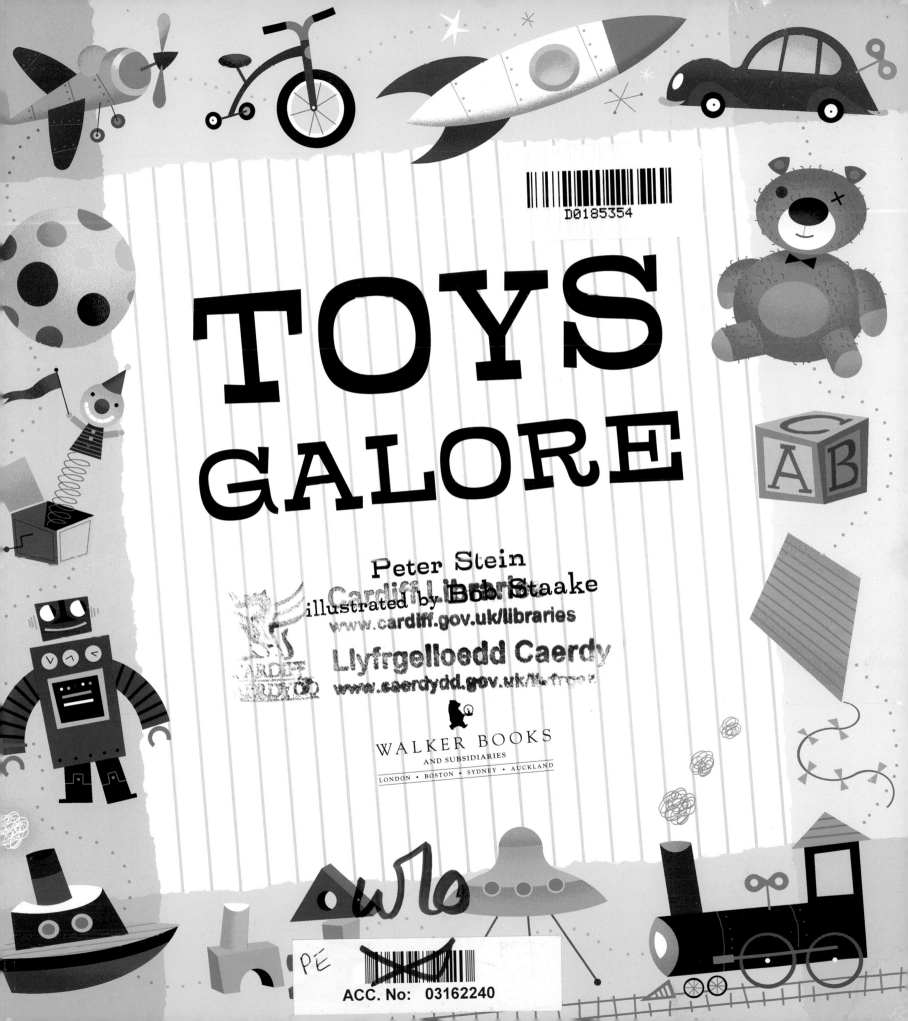

TOYS GALORE

Peter Stein

illustrated by Bob Staake

WALKER BOOKS
AND SUBSIDIARIES

LONDON • BOSTON • SYDNEY • AUCKLAND

Toys are silly.
Toys are fun.
Who loves toys?
Everyone!

THIS toy has
a lot of flair.
What other kinds
of toys are there?
It's good to know!
And nice to share.

Round toy, square toy,
earth toy, air toy.
Spring toy, string toy.
What-a-THING toy!

Small toy, tall toy,
bouncing-ball toy.
Hat toy, shoe toy.
Stretchy GOO toy!

Toys and MORE toys!
Sandy-shore toys!

Climb-it, find-it,
let's-explore toys!

A silly city
made of blocks.
A romping-robot
cardboard box.

Puppet creatures
made of socks!

Pots-and-pans toys.
Use-your-hands toys.

Sharing-secrets-
with-tin-cans toys!

Squishy clay, you're fun to play with, squeeze and squash and sculpt all day with!

Toys for teatime,
fun time, free time.
Bouncing knees are
toys for WHEEEE time!

Zippy quick
remote-control toys!

Jumpin', blastin'
rock 'n' roll toys!

Fairies, gnomes
and ugly troll toys!

Floaty, bubbly,
while-you-wash toys.

Struggling, juggling,
OH-MY-GOSH toys!

SOAP

Toys and toys and zillions MORE toys! Whirling, twirling toys-GALORE toys!

Jump toys! Ride toys!
Slip-and-slide toys!
Up-and-down and
side-to-side toys!

Toys for one
and toys for all.
Ping-pong, jacks
and basketball.

LOOK OUT BELOW!

Whew—
close call!

Creaky, squeaky
old-time race car.
Futuristic
outer-space car!
Funky go-cart
homemade chase car!

SOAP

SOAP

What are these toys?
Floaty breeze toys!
What are those toys?
Soak-your-clothes toys!

What is THAT toy?
It's a splat toy!

Toys in pairs.
Toys on stairs.

Looks like this toy
needs repairs!

Muddy toys in
messy puddles.
Snuggly toys for
hugs and cuddles.

But which toy is
the best toy ever?
The one most fun?
Most cool and clever?

It can't be found
inside a drawer
or in a box
or on the floor
or in a shop
or on a shelf.

No, this toy's found
inside *yourself*.
It's there—right now!
A toy SENSATION!

Your very own
imagination.

For Lois, Amy and Jon
P. S.

To Y
B. S.

First published 2013 by Walker Books Ltd
87 Vauxhall Walk, London SE11 5HJ

2 4 6 8 10 9 7 5 3 1

Text © 2013 Peter Stein
Illustrations © 2013 Bob Staake

The right of Peter Stein and Bob Staake to be identified as author and
illustrator respectively of this work has been asserted by them in
accordance with the Copyright, Designs and Patents Act 1988

This book has been typeset in Zalderdash

Printed in China

British Library Cataloguing in Publication Data:
a catalogue record for this book is available from the British Library

ISBN 978-1-4063-4621-3

www.walker.co.uk